ROSMARIE HAUSHERR

THE CITY GIRL WHO WENT TO SEA

FOUR WINDS PRESS   NEW YORK

. . . .

CONTENTS

Four Winds Press, Macmillan Publishing Company, 866 Third Avenue, New York, NY 10022. Collier Macmillan Canada, Inc.
First Edition   Printed in the United States of America 10 9 8 7 6 5 4 3 2 1
Library of Congress Cataloging-in-Publication Data
Hausherr, Rosmarie. The city girl who went to sea / Rosmarie Hausherr.—1st ed.   p.   cm. Summary: A ten-year-old girl from New York City learns about the traditional fishermen's way of life when she spends the summer in the remote Newfoundland fishing village of Salvage.
1. Salvage (Nfld.)—Social life and customs—Juvenile literature. 2. Fishing—Newfoundland—Salvage—Juvenile literature. [1. Newfoundland—Social life and customs. 2. Fishing—Newfoundland.] I. Title.   ISBN 0-02-743421-4
F1124.5.S25H38 1990 971.8—dc20   89-27236 CIP AC

. . . .

A
VILLAGE
FAR AWAY

THE people of Salvage have fished the cold waters of the North Atlantic Ocean for generations.

They live on the shores of an inlet, where a barrier of cliffs protects their houses and boats from the hungry sea.

The village of Salvage is tucked away on the rocky island of Newfoundland, a province of Canada. Its people live in much the same way as their great-great-grandparents from Scotland, England, and Ireland did. The men brave the sea in small fishing boats. The women care for the family, house, and garden. They are hardy, warm, and generous people who take good care of their children and look after their elders.

A few years ago, an American girl came to stay in Salvage for the summer. This is the story of her visit.

THE
CITY GIRL

ALICIA Belford had lived all ten years of her life in the shadow of tall buildings in New York City.

She shared a tiny one-room apartment with her mother and Benny, the cat.

During the winter, her cluttered home was cozy, but when spring arrived, Alicia felt closed in. Even Benny grew restless.

On mild evenings Alicia would sit with her cat on the fire escape. There she liked to read and daydream.

One day something unexpected happened: an airmail letter arrived for Alicia's mother. She read it to herself. After dinner she spread out a map that said CANADA.

"You see this island, Alicia? It's called Newfoundland. Some distant cousins, Bessie and Arthur, live there in a village called Salvage. They have three girls."

"How old are they?" Alicia wanted to know.

"Ida is about your age, Beverly is much older, and Sarah, I believe, is about two," her mother said. "I wrote to Bessie and Arthur and asked if you could possibly spend your summer vacation with them. They have answered back that they would be happy to have you."

Alicia looked at the map. Newfoundland seemed a great distance away.

"But, Mom, I would be so far away from you," Alicia said.

"I know," Mrs. Belford answered. "I want you to understand, Alicia, that you don't have to go there. But it could be a nice place to enjoy the summer. Let's think about it."

During the following weeks, Alicia and her mom talked often about Salvage. They borrowed a book from the library with pictures of Newfoundland. Alicia had endless questions.

"Do they speak English?"

"Yes, they do."

"Do they have TV? What do they eat?"

Her mother laughed. "I don't know, Alicia. I've never been there myself."

One day a letter arrived from Ida.

"Dear Alicia," it said in crooked letters, "I hope you come to Salvage. My mother says you are nice. You can have your own bedroom. Write soon, please. Love, Ida."

Alicia went to sit on the stoop. There she read the short letter over and over. She had more questions than ever. What would it be like to fly in an airplane? How would it feel living with people she had never seen before? Would the children in the village play with her?

Then she remembered the hot, crowded bus that had taken her to day camp last summer.

"Mom, I think I'll go to Salvage and stay with Ida," Alicia said when she returned to the apartment. "But what if I get homesick?"

"If that happens, we'll arrange for you to fly home earlier," Mom said. "And I'll call you every week." She hugged Alicia. "I'm proud of my big girl."

. . . .

ON a humid July day, Alicia kissed her mother good-bye and boarded a big plane. In Gander, a friendly airport employee brought Alicia to a bus outside the small terminal.

"This young lady has to get off at Glovertown Junction, where a relative named Arthur Heffern will meet her," the woman instructed the bus driver.

"I'll see to that," the driver said. From her seat right in front, Alicia eyed the passing forests and lakes with curiosity.

A friendly man with a mustache met the bus. "You must be Alicia," he said. "You can call me Uncle Arthur," he added as he helped her into his green pickup truck.

They chatted about her long trip. But Alicia was having a hard time keeping her eyes open. She had not slept much the night before.

Safely seated in Uncle Arthur's truck, she fell asleep.

Alicia woke up when the wheels hit a bump in the dirt road. "Where am I?" she asked.

"We're just about home," Uncle Arthur said. Alicia peered with astonishment at the clear water of Bonavista Bay. They approached the first houses of a village as the sun went down.

"This is Salvage—and here is our home." Uncle Arthur swung the truck into a driveway.

The family came outside to meet Alicia.

"This is Ida," Uncle Arthur said. That was the girl in front of him. "And here are Sarah and Beverly."

"I'm your Aunt Bessie," a friendly-looking woman said, "and this is Uncle Pearce." That was the tall man in the doorway.

"We're glad you came," added Grandma, who wore a flowery dress. She smiled, and Grandpa nodded.

"You must be starved, Alicia!" Aunt Bessie said, and they all took her into the house.

. . . .

A FULL TABLE
AND
A NEW VILLAGE

ALICIA could hear the swishing sound of water. Was it raining? she wondered as she opened her eyes. Sunlight danced on the wall.

She looked around the unfamiliar bedroom, jumped out of bed, and ran to the window.

On the far side of a dirt road, water washed against a rocky shore. White boats slept lazily in the sun. Well-groomed houses stood on small patches of land along the road.

The door opened slowly. The aroma of oatmeal sneaked into the bedroom, followed by Ida.

"Alicia, you're up! All my friends came to the house early to see you, but you were still asleep. You want breakfast?"

"Yes, please."

In the warm kitchen, Ida's grandma was busy with pots and pans. "Did you sleep well, my dear?" she asked, dishing oatmeal into a bowl.

"Yes, thank you," Alicia said. Ida brought jam, canned milk, butter, and toast to the table.

Alicia didn't like oatmeal very much, but she felt too shy to say so. Ida noticed and said, "I eat my oatmeal with jam on top."

Alicia tried it. "It's good!" she said, and the girls smiled at each other.

After breakfast, the girls went outdoors.

"Come back for dinner. Your father will be home today," Grandma said as they headed out the door.

"Ida, can we stay outside till five o'clock?" Alicia asked in surprise.

"No, we have to be back by twelve."

"But that's lunch," Alicia pointed out.

"No, lunch is a late-night snack."

"Then what do you call the evening meal?"

"Oh," said Ida, "that's supper."

As Ida and Alicia walked down the road, they spotted a group of girls playing on a wharf.

"Alicia is here!" Ida yelled. They came running. Alicia met her next-door neighbor, Eileen Brown, who was eleven. Marlene, Lucy, and Marie Heffern were sisters who lived up the road.

. . . .

"IDAAAAA! Aliciaaaa!"

"That's my mother," Ida said. She led Alicia back to the house, where the family was sitting around the kitchen table.

Alicia was placed next to Uncle Arthur. He was a forest ranger, she learned, and off duty for the day. Aunt Bessie was looking around the table to make sure nothing was missing. Next to her sat Uncle Pearce. To his left were Grandma and Grandpa, and with their backs to the window were Beverly, Ida, and Sarah.

Grandma blessed the food on the table. The girls were hungry, and the hearty soup tasted delicious with homemade bread. Pickles and coleslaw were passed around. Dessert was cake or bread pudding, with tea.

The Hefferns, who had never visited a large city, wanted to know about New York.

"Do you live in Manhattan, where all the skyscrapers are?" Aunt Bessie asked.

Alicia swallowed her cake and nodded.

"Then you live on an island, too," Uncle Arthur said. Alicia looked at him, surprised.

"Yes, I forgot. Because of all those big buildings I hardly ever see the water." She described how she lived with her mother and told them about school, her friends, and the things she liked to do: ice skating, shopping, visiting museums. Used to quiet meals alone with her mother, she enjoyed the lively family dinner.

Ida and Alicia were drying dishes when Ida's best friend, Roxane, and her brother, Ian, stopped by.

"Why don't you take Alicia around shore?" Aunt Bessie suggested. "That's what we call the only road through the village," she explained.

Salvage stretched in a half circle around a saltwater harbor that looked like a big lake. Behind the houses, rocky hills rose against the sky. The air was crisp and salty.

"Where do you go to school?" Alicia asked as they walked down the road.

"We're bussed to Eastport, the next town," Ian said. "What about you?"

"My mom walks me to P.S. 41. My school has almost nine hundred students."

"Wow! We have only 248," Roxane said.

Alicia motioned to the water. "Do you go swimming?"

"Yes, but the water is freezing," Ida said, pretending to make her teeth chatter.

"My big cousin dives off that wharf. See the store over there, Alicia?" Ian said.

She saw nothing but a wooden shack. "Is that a grocery store?" she asked.

"Grocery store!" Ian laughed, and explained to Alicia that a store was a shed where a fisherman stored his gear. The wooden platform attached to the store was the wharf, where the fisherman moored and unloaded his boat.

Alicia grinned. "I'll show you New York someday," she said.

At the far end of the harbor, they stopped and looked across the water at the village. From a distance Alicia could clearly recognize the dark red fishermen's stores on the edge of the water, and behind them, the white painted houses where people lived.

"We could show Alicia the fish plant," Ida suggested.

"Does it have flowers?" Alicia asked.

For a moment they looked puzzled. Then they burst into laughter.

"It's . . . it's . . . it's a fish factory," Ian said, holding his belly. Alicia had to laugh, too.

"I'm hungry. Let's go to my house," Roxane suggested.

The smell of freshly baked bread welcomed them into the kitchen.

"Mom," Roxane said, "this is Alicia, our new friend."

. . . .

KNITS, NETS, AND BOATS

IDA'S house reminded Alicia of the ones she used to draw when she was little. The roof sloped steeply and the windows were evenly spaced around the door.

"It's fun to live in a house," she said to Ida at breakfast the next morning.

"Why?" Ida asked.

"Because I'm used to living in one room, and here I can run upstairs and downstairs."

"Where do you cook?" Ida wanted to know.

"We have a small kitchenette in one corner."

"A kitchenette!" Ida repeated. "Where is your wood stove?"

Alicia laughed. "We don't have one. It would take up all the kitchen space."

After breakfast, Ida took Alicia to the Browns' house next door. Violet Brown welcomed them into a cheerful kitchen.

"Come and sit with me, Alicia," she said, picking up her knitting. The wool glided smoothly through Violet's fingers. The needles clicked rhythmically. A beautiful sweater in pink, white, and burgundy was growing from her skilled hands. Alicia, who had just learned how to knit, watched with awe. She usually struggled with slipping needles, too much yarn, and not enough fingers.

Violet wanted to hear about Alicia's trip. While listening, she glanced through the window from time to time at the place across the cove where two men were painting a boat.

"That's my husband, Andrew, and our son, Andy," Violet said proudly. "Andrew is a fisherman."

"Where's Eileen?" Ida wanted to know.

"She went to the grocery store."

Ida nudged Alicia. "Let's play outside."

"Come by any time, my dears," Violet said as the girls left.

Outside the Browns' house, Ian was biking dare-devil style around a woodpile.

"Hi," he shouted. "You want to watch them pull a long-liner out of the water?"

"What's a long-liner?" Alicia asked after he stopped with a skid.

"It's a big fishing boat with a deck, a mast, radar, sonar, and shortwave radio."

Alicia had noticed a large number of boats along the shore of the village—like cars in the city.

"People must have lots of money to buy so many boats," she said as they walked along.

"They don't buy the boats; they build them," Ian said. "In the winter, when it's too cold for fishing."

"How do they know how to build a boat?" Alicia asked.

Ian shrugged. "They just know."

. . . .

"HI, Uncle Gar," Ida shouted to a fisherman who was mending a net with a giant wooden needle.

"You must be the city girl, eh?" Uncle Gar said to Alicia.

She nodded. "Why does the net have holes?"

"I suppose it got torn on the rocks in a storm."

"A big shark ripped it up," Ian suggested.

Alicia asked apprehensively, "Are there sharks in the water here?"

Gar Heffern laughed. "There aren't many in these waters, but off and on we see whales out in the ocean."

"Look, the long-liner is coming out of the water!" Ian shouted, and pointed to the other side of the cove. Without waiting for Ida and Alicia, he took off on his bicycle.

By the time the girls arrived at the dry dock, the keel of the *Bryon Bay* was halfway up the ramp. A noisy motor turned the wheels and cables that slowly pulled the liner out of the water.

Ian was leaning against his bike. "Someday I'll have a long-liner like that," he said.

"Could I go out on the ocean in a boat?" Alicia asked.

"They don't take ladies," Ian said, and made a funny face. Alicia hoped he was only joking.

GRANDPA was working quietly on a fishnet in the kitchen when Ida and Alicia came home.

"You know how to make nets, too?" Alicia said in surprise.

"I daresay. I've knitted them all my life," Grandpa answered proudly.

Alicia watched the old man. Making a net was like knitting very loosely. She remembered her own knitting, still packed in the suitcase, and decided to go outside and add a few rows.

The afternoon sun warmed Alicia's skin as she sat on a pile of silver-colored wood planks near the water.

"Alicia!" Ida called. Alicia looked up from her knitting and saw her friend running toward her.

"Guess what? Mom bought fabric for my flower girl dress. I'm going to be in my cousin Lindsay's wedding. Come and see."

The girls walked to the house together. "You're lucky, Ida. I've never been a flower girl," Alicia said.

"If you could stay with us long enough, you would be one," Ida told her. "We have lots of weddings in the village."

THE LETTER

ALICIA had promised her mother to write often. The next day she sat down with a pen and her pink stationery. "Dear Mom," she scribbled, "I like Salvage. Everybody is very nice. Ida is my best friend. I have lots of new friends. I miss you. How is Benny?" She chewed on her pen. There was so much to tell.

In the end it took a few days to complete the letter. At last Alicia dressed up in her favorite summer outfit, ready to go to the post office.

"Can I go by myself?" she asked Aunt Bessie.

"Of course, my dear. You're perfectly safe."

Alicia had just walked past the first bend in the road when she heard screaming and laughter. Marie, her friend Colleen, and Ian were perched on the edge of a wharf, casting fishing lines.

"Alicia! Come jig with us," Ian shouted.

"Okay!" She climbed onto the wood, which was coated with fish scales.

They took turns holding the fishing lines.

"Alicia, you have to jig a bit," Colleen instructed her.

"What's jigging?" Alicia asked.

Colleen jerked the line. "This makes the fish snap for the bait on the hook," she explained.

"A fish!" Marie yelled. A chorus of excited screams echoed among the houses.

Alicia jumped up. "What are you going to do?"

Marie unhooked the flapping animal. "It's too bony to eat," she said, and threw the fish back into the water.

Eventually Alicia remembered her letter. Her dress looking a bit crumpled now, she left her friends and took off along the dirt road. There was little traffic. Cars drove slowly to keep down the dust.

The post office looked like any other house in the village, except for a red-and-white Canada postal sign on the front. Alicia followed the gravel path to the back, where she faced two white doors. Which one led to the post office? Slowly she opened the one to the left and peeked into the Hancock family kitchen. She closed it and tried the other door.

In a small room, the postmistress, Belle Hancock, smiled at her from the only teller window. "So, I heard you sneak into my kitchen!" she said to Alicia, who blushed.

"I thought the whole building was the post office, like in the city," Alicia said.

"In rural villages the post office is often just a room at the postmaster's house," Belle explained.

Alicia handed over her letter. Belle attached a flower stamp.

"Do you have others with flowers? I collect stamps," Alicia said.

"Come in, I'll show them to you."

Alicia crawled through the mailbag door. Belle gave her six floral stamps. "A souvenir from Canada," she said.

"Thank you!"

"How about giving me a hand with the mailbags? I've been the postmistress for over thirty years, but I can still use some help now and then." Belle opened the large canvas bag filled with packages. Alicia's job was to hand each one to her. As the sack emptied, she reached deep for the last parcel and almost tipped into the bag.

"That's how we trap naughty kids and ship them off—in empty postal sacks," Belle remarked.

Alicia looked, startled, at Belle, who grinned.

Children came to pick up the mail for their families and were surprised to see Alicia amidst the canvas bags. One customer purchased a money order. Roy Lane, who needed a government form, inquired if Belle had hired a new postal employee.

Her customers exchanged the latest village news with Belle. Nobody seemed to be rushing. Alicia stuffed junk mail into boxes, one for each of the sixty-four families.

"How about a sandwich, Alicia? I'm closing for dinner. And here—a love letter from your boyfriend!" Belle handed her a light blue envelope with Mom's unmistakable handwriting on it.

LATER that afternoon, Alicia stopped by Violet's house. On the table lay her knitting.

"Andrew found it on the woodpile," Violet said. "Are you knitting a scarf?"

"No, a pot holder. I don't have much wool."

"I have plenty of that," Violet said, and brought out a box of leftover yarn. Alicia rummaged happily and chose blue and pink wool. Violet cast twenty-six stitches on for her.

"My mom will be surprised to get a new scarf," Alicia said, knitting slowly. "I'll keep it a secret—I hope." Violet's own needles clicked as she listened to the news from Alicia's letter.

TURNIPS
AND
BERRIES

AFTER a string of sunny July days, heavy clouds sailed inland. Raindrops drummed on roofs. The kitchen, with its warm wood stove, became the heart of every house.

The children took turns visiting one another. They played board and card games and put puzzles together, or watched one of the few available TV programs.

On the third day of rain, Alicia was playing Scrabble at Lucy and Marie's house. She put the last two letters on the board. "That makes ninety-seven points. I won," she said.

"Not again." Marie was annoyed. "You think you're so smart, don't you?"

"No," Alicia said quickly, "but I play Scrabble with Mom."

"Oh, you and your mommy," Marie said, mimicking Alicia. "I'm such a smarty from the city, right, Mommy?" The other girls laughed.

Alicia got up and ran to Aunt Bessie's house. She hid under the covers in her bedroom and cried.

After supper, Marie's big sisters brought her over to Ida's house so she could let Alicia know that she was sorry. Now they were friends again.

. . . .

FINALLY, bright sunshine dried the well-washed village. Aunt Bessie sent Alicia to return a ladle to Aunt Mary Heffern. All these Heffern families! Alicia found them very confusing.

She was happy to be outdoors again. On the way to Aunt Mary's house she twirled the ladle like a cheerleader's baton. She found Mary working in the garden.

"Hi, Mary. Here's your ladle," Alicia said.

"Thank you, my dear."

"What are these?" She pointed to the leafy green plants that Mary was weeding.

"Turnips," Mary said. "I cook them with parsnips, carrots, potatoes, cabbages, and a piece of salt beef or salt pork."

"I don't like cooked vegetables," Alicia said. "I eat them raw."

"Like a rabbit, eh?" Mary said, and smiled.

Alicia helped with the weeding. Mary told her that when she was a girl, the only vegetables eaten by every family in the village were those they grew in their own gardens.

"What else did you have to eat?" Alicia asked.

"The men brought home fresh or salted fish. In the winter they hunted rabbit, waterfowl, or moose. With the money they earned from fishing, they bought groceries twice a year: butter, flour, molasses, sugar, tea, salt beef, tobacco. With luck, Father would bring back a bushel of apples for the children."

For Alicia, used to buying everything in a store, such a life seemed hard. "I guess you didn't have much candy," she remarked.

"No, I suppose not, but Mother baked sweet buns, molasses cookies, and mighty good pies," Mary answered.

They had reached the end of the row. Mary pulled a few small carrots and handed them to Alicia. "For my city rabbit," she said.

"Here you are, Alicia!" Marlene shouted from the far end of the picket fence. "You want to come berry picking?"

"I'd love to," Alicia said happily.

"I brought you a jar," Marlene said, and off they went to the top of a nearby hill. There were Ida, Ian, and Roxane, who had descended on a raspberry patch.

"Yummy!" Ida said, filling her mouth instead of the jar.

Roxane, full of ambition, had brought a half-gallon bucket.

"Who can pick the most berries?" Marlene said.

Alicia scratched her hand and arm reaching for the red berries. They often fell to the ground when she touched them, but she picked steadily.

"We picked blackberries in early summer," Marlene told her. "After the raspberries will come blueberries and then partridgeberries." Berries, she explained, were the only native fruit in much of Newfoundland's coastal areas. Fruit trees didn't grow well because of the harsh winds.

"Let's compare," Marlene yelled.

Ian reappeared from behind a rock. He opened his bucket and *whupp*! A shiny frog jumped into the grass, barely missing Marlene's overalls.

Roxane had eaten most of her berries, and Ida's red-stained lips did not promise a big harvest either. But Alicia's glass jar was almost full, and Marlene had picked a quart.

At Ida's house, Alicia had noticed, someone was always home. Ida never had to put up with babysitters, as Alicia did. Many of Alicia's Salvage friends lived with their grandparents or next to them. Alicia felt a bit envious and wished her grandparents did not live so far away—across the ocean in Ireland.

Alicia liked the old people in Salvage. They were kind, patient listeners, and they seemed to have an inexhaustible supply of cookies—and pie.

"Let's bring them home," Ida suggested. Marlene stayed behind to pick another quart.

"Look, Grandma," Ida shouted as the two girls burst into the kitchen.

"That's just enough berries for a pie," Grandma said with a smile.

A COLD DIP
AND
TINY STITCHES

EILEEN Brown and Alicia were cooling off in the shade when Marlene showed up with a handful of children. "We're going swimming, to Back Beach. Are you coming?"

Alicia and Eileen dashed home for their bathing suits. Clutching their beach towels, they filed down a narrow path, toward the sea.

The older children helped the younger ones climb down a cliff to a gravel beach.

Eileen waded into the water up to her waist. "It's great!" she screamed.

Alicia dipped her toes in. "It's *freezing*!"

By now everybody else was in the water. Alicia was worried they would call her a sissy. "Don't splash, pleeeease," she pleaded, walking gingerly toward her friends. At that moment she slipped and plunged into the water with a piercing screech.

Marie showed Alicia how to float on soft waves traveling toward the beach. The children chased and splashed one another. Pinching their noses shut, they dove for colorful gravel and small shells. Alicia tasted the salt on her lips. When she was chilled, she left the water.

"Oh, no! My towel is wet," she cried. She had dropped it at the water's edge, and the incoming tide had quietly encroached on it. Laury, one of the younger girls, shared her beach towel with Alicia.

All the children dried themselves on the hot gravel beach. As soon as they were warmed up, they went back into the water, in and out all afternoon. They returned home very hungry.

After supper, Alicia helped Ida's sister Beverly do the dishes.

"Do you go swimming?" Alicia asked.

"Yes, sometimes," Beverly said.

"Do Aunt Bessie and Uncle Arthur swim?"

"No, they never learned to. None of the adults in Salvage can swim."

"But shouldn't the fishermen know how? I mean, in case they fall into the water by mistake," Alicia wondered.

"It would be difficult to swim in boots and heavy clothing. The ocean water is so icy. I daresay swimming wouldn't help much." Beverly noticed Alicia's concerned expression and added, "The fishermen know the sea and their boats well, and they are careful."

"Is your boyfriend a fisherman?" Alicia asked.

"He is," Beverly said with a proud smile.

WHEN the dishes were done, Alicia went to visit Ida's great-great-aunt, who was called Aunt Mary Jane by all the villagers out of respect. She lived in a small yellow house just above Mary Heffern's garden. For much of the day, she sat at her living room window, observing her neighbors' activities with great interest while knitting or sewing.

From the shaded porch, Aunt Mary Jane was watching Alicia climb the path to her house in the evening sunshine.

"I've seen you from my window many times," the old woman said with a welcoming smile. "Come sit with me, my dear."

"This is beautiful!" Alicia said, sliding her hand over the spread on Aunt Mary Jane's lap.

"It's a quilt I made a long time ago."

"Why did you cut the fabric into such small pieces?"

"Well, my love, in the old days, fabric was hard to come by. I saved every scrap of clothing and cut them up. Then I stitched them into squares and sewed them into a quilt on my machine."

Aunt Mary Jane turned a corner of the spread over. "See, I covered the back with flour sacks." Alicia nodded.

"My quilt brings back memories—happy ones and a few sad ones, too. This light blue square is from my daughter Barbara's graduation dress. And here, the red-checkered cotton comes from one of my husband's shirts, bless his soul."

From a shoebox Aunt Mary Jane pulled an unfinished square. The stitches were tiny.

"It would take me a hundred years to make a quilt," Alicia said.

Aunt Mary Jane chuckled. "I feel a bit of a draft on my back. Let's go inside."

In her kitchen she brought the kettle to a boil. They drank tea from porcelain cups and ate raisin buns. Aunt Mary Jane was eager to hear how Alicia liked Salvage.

"I saw you berry pickin' the other day. I used to pick for years. Now my old legs won't carry me anymore. But I'll tell you my secret berry patch." She lowered her voice. "The old cemetery."

. . . .

THE hot Sunday turned into a mild night. Uncle Arthur took Alicia and Ida outside and pointed to the sky. In the darkness thousands of stars blinked and sparkled brightly.

Alicia had never seen the stars so clearly. In the city, with its many lights, they were invisible to her. She listened, awestruck, as Uncle Arthur pointed out the Big Dipper, the Little Dipper, the Great Bear, the North Star, and the Milky Way.

At last, swarms of bloodthirsty mosquitoes drove them indoors.

. . . .

A SMALL
SEA
MONSTER

IN the morning Ida left for a week's vacation in St. John's, the capital of Newfoundland. She was bubbling over with excitement.

"I'll go shopping for white shoes with my cousin, and she'll sew my long dress for the wedding. It's only two weeks away, you know."

"I'll miss you," Alicia remarked.

"You can play with all my toys," Ida said.

Instead of playing indoors, Alicia ambled over to the Browns'. The door of the fish store was open. In the dim light, Alicia saw Andrew Brown repairing something. The wooden shack was stacked high with barrels and all kinds of fishing gear, including buoys, nets, and traps.

Andrew carried a wooden trap outside.

"Is this a birdcage?" Alicia asked.

Andrew laughed. "No, this is a lobster pot. I use it for lobster fishing."

"How do you catch a lobster?"

Andrew took a puff on his pipe. "Tomorrow morning I'll check a few pots. If the water is calm, you can come along."

A light drizzle moistened the air the following day, but the water was quiet. After breakfast, Alicia hurried over to the Browns' house.

"You better wear these, Alicia." Andrew handed her a life jacket and Eileen's yellow rain slicker. He was dressed in a black rubber coat and pants, heavy boots, and a rain hat.

At his wharf, the fisherman loaded buckets into his boat and helped Alicia climb in. The boat was slippery, and it rocked in the water. Andrew started the engine and untied the lines that moored the boat to the wharf. Violet Brown waved from the kitchen window.

Tuck . . . tuck . . . slowly the fisherman steered the boat between barnacle-encrusted rocks into the waters of the harbor, working his way cautiously along the cliffs.

Alicia sat motionless. The only boat ride she had taken before was on the small lake in Central Park. She was afraid the boat would tilt if she leaned over to gaze into the dark green water.

They had passed the swimming cove when Alicia sighted a floating piece of wood. Andrew maneuvered the boat close. He grabbed the stick with a metal hook called a gaff and lifted the marker out of the water. With his hands he pulled on the attached rope until a lobster pot surfaced. Andrew hoisted it into the boat. Empty! Alicia was disappointed.

Andrew slipped a piece of fish over a stick inside the trap for bait and swung it overboard.

"Andrew, how do you know which traps are yours?" Alicia asked as they set off a short distance to the next marker. He showed her the painted initial and told her that for generations, Salvage fishermen had placed their pots in the same spots.

A lobster sat in the next trap, looking like a small sea monster with its long antennas, thin legs, armored body, and black pinhead eyes. Alicia moved closer when Andrew removed the animal. He kept his fingers away from the powerful claws.

"A small fellow," the fisherman said. He measured it, and, to Alicia's surprise, threw it back into the water. "I can't sell undersized lobsters or females with eggs," Andrew explained.

When all the lobster pots had been checked, they returned to Andrew's wharf with seven live lobsters and half a dozen traps. The lobsters were kept in the water in a floating box.

"How many pots do you have?" Alicia asked.

"I suppose about sixty-five." Andrew moved a broken one to a separate pile. "These I'll repair during winter."

When Alicia thanked her neighbor for taking her along, he said, "Come to the house for a drop of soup."

"What do lobsters eat?" Alicia asked as she waited for her pea soup to cool.

"Clams, small fish. Anything they can grab with their claws from their hiding spot, in the sand or under rocks." Andrew buttered a slice of bread. "Not many people know that in the summer, a lobster splits its shell and crawls out of it, like a snake that sheds its skin. It's called moulting. Lobsters are protected by law until they grow a new hard shell. That's why I have to stop lobster fishing soon."

After dinner, Violet cooked two fresh lobsters for relatives who were arriving soon from mainland Canada. Andrew made himself comfortable on the narrow daybed near the table.

At first, Alicia had thought it funny that Salvage people had a bed in the kitchen. But fishermen like Andrew, who rose early, took short naps after meals. They could rest on the daybed in their work clothes.

Alicia inspected the cooked lobsters. Their grayish blue color had changed to a fiery red. She felt sorry for the little sea monsters.

"I'd rather eat an omelette," she said.

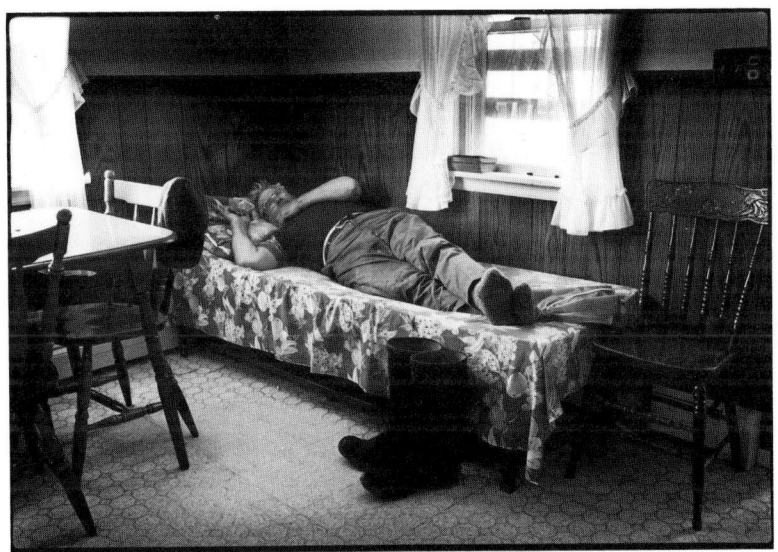

. . . .

THE
GATE

ONE early August afternoon, while Ida was still away, Alicia decided to pick a bouquet of the bluebells she had noticed in the grass behind the post office. But when she reached the meadow, she discovered that the flowers had withered. Hoping to find others, Alicia followed a path that led into the hills.

She walked over short, dry grass and mossy rocks, leaving the houses of the village behind. The path narrowed, winding through scruffy brush and wind-crippled firs. When the trees loomed over her, Alicia decided to turn back. At that moment she spotted a rusty gate.

The gate opened with a grating sound. *Whhrrr,* a bird fled from a bush. Alicia held her breath. Her heart beat wildly. Something white glistened beyond the trees. She hesitated, then pushed through the prickly fir branches. She was standing in an overgrown cemetery.

"I found Aunt Mary Jane's secret berry patch!" she said aloud.

A gravestone with a small cross leaned precariously to one side.

IN MEMORY

M A R Y - A N N   B R O W N

AGED 5 YEARS AND 3 MONTHS

Alicia wondered why the little girl had died.

Another stone rested flat on the earth. She brushed the leaves off. The last names on the headstones were those of her friends: Heffern, Brown, Lane, Hancock. . . .

The sun had vanished and the light seemed dim. Alicia looked for the raspberries that Aunt Mary Jane had mentioned. But only low bushes with tiny green berries grew between the graves.

Wrummmm, wrummmm. Alicia spun around. A wall of black clouds had crawled over the back of the hill. A blue flash of lightning was followed by another *wrummmm* of thunder.

Alicia dashed among the stones and through the bushes to the cemetery gate. The fir branches felt like arms trying to hold her back. As fast as she could, she sped down the narrow path. Large raindrops landed on her scratched arms and legs. She had just made it to the door of the first house beyond the meadow when the water came down in buckets. She darted inside.

"My goodness, Alicia, you look like you saw a ghost," Belle Hancock said when the girl unexpectedly appeared in her kitchen.

"I almost did," Alicia said.

FRESH EGGS
AND
A BROOM

ROXANE'S family was one of the few in the village that raised chickens. When Alicia was sent there to buy a dozen eggs, Roxane took her to a small stable at the end of the garden.

Roxane entered the chicken pen with a tray of fresh water. During school vacation, she explained, she and Ian fed the animals. "I wish we still had our two horses and our sheep," she said. "But not enough grass grows here to make hay for the winter." She returned with a hat full of eggs, one of them still warm.

On her way home, Alicia passed the house where Heber Heffern, Ida's uncle, lived with his family. Heber was kneeling outside the door on the wooden deck that was called the bridge. Alicia stopped and asked what he was doing.

Heber looked up. "I'm cutting a piece of birch for a broom."

"A broom! Can you make a broom from a piece of wood?" Alicia asked.

"Yeah, you can watch."

Heber sharpened his knife. With the birch across his legs, he sat comfortably in the morning sun outside his house, Alicia by his side. First he sliced into the end of the wood. Then he lifted the small wood shaving with blade and thumb and peeled it back about the length of his hand. He rotated the piece of birch and continued stripping the wood to the same point. With his left hand he held the shavings down.

 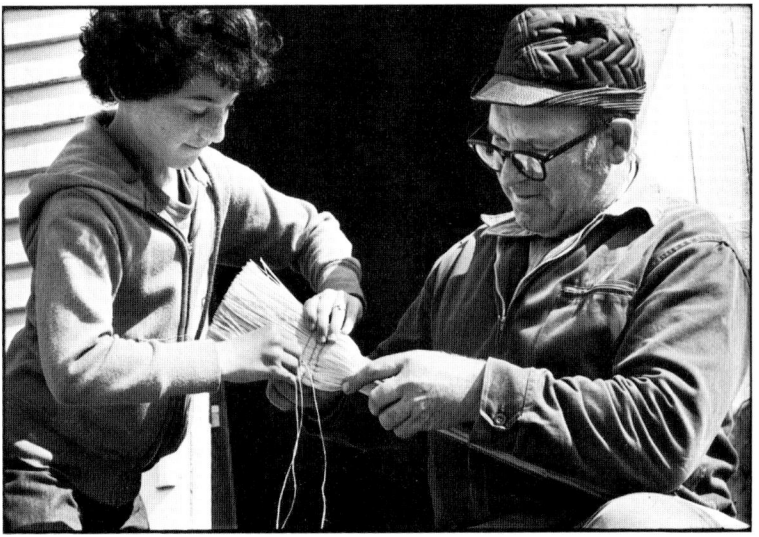

Alicia was fascinated. "It looks so easy," she commented

"You think so, eh? I've messed up quite a few. The trick is, the wood has to be green."

"But it's white."

Heber explained that "green" wood was freshly cut and still wet. "How was lobster fishing the other day?" he asked.

"Great," Alicia said. "You think I could go out in a fishing boat?"

"You want to be a fisherwoman, eh?"

"No, but I'd like to see the ocean outside the harbor," Alicia said.

Uncle Pearce and Sarah stopped by on their way to the grocery store. "Fine day today," he said.

When people met on the road in Salvage, Alicia had observed, they always exchanged a few words about the weather and a bit of news.

Alicia listened to the two men talk about Lindsay's upcoming wedding. He was Heber's oldest son, she realized. At times she had difficulties understanding Salvage people. Words beginning with a vowel, like *apples,* were pronounced with an *h*—"happles." A mosquito was a "nipper," a photograph was a "snap," and "a time" meant having a party. If Alicia couldn't figure out what someone said to her, she just smiled.

"I'd better go," Uncle Pearce said. "Good day."

While he was talking, Heber had sliced the end off the stick. With a hammer he pounded the shavings. Then he stitched them into shape with a big needle and green twine.

Alicia was impressed. "It's a broom!"

"The handle still needs carving and sanding."

"I wish I could bring a broom like that home to my mom, but it's too long for my suitcase. Oh, the *eggs*!" Alicia had forgotten all about them.

"I suppose I could make one with a shorter handle," Heber suggested. But Alicia was already halfway down the hill.

Her late return with the eggs delayed the baking of a cake. Though nobody scolded her, Alicia felt a bit guilty. Later in the day, she disappeared to a quiet spot.

She missed her mom and wished she could cuddle Benny and hear his comforting purr. But she liked being in Salvage, too. Everybody wanted her to be happy. Her feelings were confusing!

Every Friday evening, her mother called. That was just two days away. And Ida would be back soon.

"I guess I'll stay here a bit longer," Alicia said to herself.

· · · · · · · · · · · · · ·

WIND
AND
FISH

A SLEEPY lull hung over the village. On the bridge outside the house, Alicia was absorbed in a book. The wind played with her curly hair and pulled on the pages of her book like an impatient friend.

In this coastal village, the wind was ever-present. The fishermen watched it closely. A whispering breeze might grow within a short time into a storm, chasing clouds and whipping waves into "white horses." That's what the villagers called the white foam on the waves.

Alicia looked up from her book and saw Marie's mother struggling with the flapping dry wash on the clothesline. Alicia hurried over to help. She grabbed the swaying rope and held onto it. That made it easier for her neighbor to remove the laundry and hang a new batch of wet clothes.

Alicia loved the fresh smell of wind- and sundried wash. It was so different from the clothes her mother tumble dried at the Laundromat.

Marie's brother Kenny dashed by on his bike.

"Kenny!" his mother shouted. "I want you to go to the fish plant." Too late!

"I can go," Alicia volunteered.

"Thank you, my dear. Ask Fred Heffern if he's brought back crab's legs for Lindsay's wedding dinner."

Alicia walked along the familiar road. She gazed across the water to the passage between the cliffs, catching a glimpse of the sea. She was curious about the ocean beyond the harbor and still hoped to be taken out in a fishing boat. "I'll ask Fred," she decided.

AT the fish plant, Alicia spotted Fred Heffern's long-liner at the end of the crowded wharf. She threaded her way across the slippery planks, careful not to step in fish waste. Fred, who was Mary Heffern's husband, fished together with his brother, Eliol.

Alicia gave him the message. The two men were unloading fish into wooden boxes. The fish odor was strong. Alicia wrinkled her nose.

Once the hull of the boat was empty, Eliol hosed down the long-liner with fresh water. Fred climbed onto the wharf. With a sharp knife he began cleaning cod on a sturdy table.

The first time Alicia had seen a fish being gutted, she had nearly been sick. It had not occurred to her that a fish, like any animal—even like herself—had a heart, kidneys, a stomach, and intestines. Fish for her was a clean, white, frozen piece of fillet or breaded sticks in a box from the supermarket. She had never cared much for seafood, but she rather liked Grandma's Fish and Brewis, a Newfoundland dish of codfish mashed with hard biscuits.

"Do you think I could go out in a boat, Fred?" Alicia asked.

"I suppose so," Fred answered, "but we couldn't take you. We fish far out, all day long. You would get seasick."

Alicia understood, but she was still a bit disappointed.

"What do you do with all the fish?" she asked.

"It gets packed on ice here at the fish plant and trucked to mainland Canada or the U.S. Before they had ice machines, the fish had to be salted or dried."

Accompanied by flocks of screeching sea gulls, more long-liners were gliding into the harbor with their catches. Late afternoon was a busy time at the fish plant. Moored in double rows, the colorful boats danced gently to the rhythm of the waves. The fishermen, clad in overalls, joked good-humoredly with one another while unloading or gutting fish.

"I'd better get back for supper," Alicia said.

"If you'd like, you can cross the harbor with us," Fred suggested.

ALICIA was happy to see that Ida had come home. Her friend took her to the living room. "Look!" she said, pointing to her flower girl dress.

"It's beautiful!" Alicia exclaimed.

Ida paraded around the room in her new white shoes. "This is for you, Alicia, to wear at the wedding." Ida handed her a pretty pair of white knee socks.

"You mean I'm going to the wedding, too?"

"Of course. You're one of the family."

"But I don't have a fancy dress," Alicia said.

"Your nice red one with the little flowers will be fine," Aunt Bessie assured her.

. . . .

IN the village, the upcoming wedding of Heber Heffern's oldest son was of interest to young and old. That the bride was from New Brunswick and spoke French made it all the more exciting. The Hefferns had plenty of relatives and neighbors to help with the preparations. Traditionally, the women cooked the meal and served it at the reception.

The day before the wedding, a big turkey was roasting in the oven at Ida's house. Grandma was preparing a large bowl of her tasty potato salad, while Aunt Bessie ironed white shirts and dresses for her family.

Ida and Alicia studied the bridal section of the newly arrived mail-order catalogue.

"I'd like a wedding gown that's *long* in the back." Ida made a sweeping gesture.

"I think you'd have a problem on the dirt road," Alicia said, and the girls burst into laughter.

. . . .

A
WEDDING

THE house was quiet on the morning of the wedding. Grandma and Beverly were at the hairdresser's, and Ida was over at Heber's house. Aunt Bessie was helping at the hall.

St. Stephen's Hall was once the local school. Now it served as the town hall, where meetings, dances, dart games, and wedding receptions took place.

Ian and Roxane lived next door to the hall. They were milling around the open door when Alicia delivered a bag from Grandma. Aunt Bessie and her neighbors, their hair in curlers, were putting finishing touches to the hall for the reception. Twisted streamers and lilac and pink paper carnations lent charm to the plain room.

Outside Heber's house, a crowd of curious youngsters watched the comings and goings of wedding guests. Inside, family members and neighbors, who usually were dressed in plaid shirts and cotton dresses, mingled in dark suits, long gowns, and rhinestones. Alicia found Ida in the living room.

"Want to see the bride?" Ida asked. They peeked through a half-opened bedroom door.

"Isn't she beautiful?" Ida whispered.

"You look pretty, too," Alicia said.

Until it was time to join the wedding party, Alicia played Monopoly with Ian and Roxane. About three o'clock the two girls walked to Heber's house.

"Do you have a boyfriend, Alicia?" Roxane asked.

"Not really," Alicia said, and blushed. "But there's a boy in my class who's cute."

"Ian could be your boyfriend. He likes you," Roxane suggested.

"He's nice," Alicia said, "but I'm going back to New York soon."

"I daresay that wouldn't be practical."

The wedding party emerged from the house to the sound of church bells. A mischievous wind immediately rearranged hairdos and whirled the bride's veil into the air. The party took refuge in the waiting cars. The children ran alongside the slow-moving, horn-blowing procession of decorated vehicles to the church.

Wearing her pretty dress, flowers in her hair, Ida walked slowly to the front of the church, arm in arm with a cousin. The harmonium played the wedding march, missing a note here and there. Then the bride came down the aisle and met the groom and minister in front of the congregation. All eyes were focused on her veil-covered face.

The church was packed. The service seemed endless to Alicia and her fidgety friends.

Outside the church, the newly married couple was congratulated, hugged and kissed, and sprinkled with rice. But the cool wind made everybody move quickly to the hall, where the celebration continued.

St. Stephen's Hall was filled to the last chair. Toasts were offered, speeches made, and photographs taken. Then the traditional meal of turkey was served.

After the meal the children slipped outdoors and played hide-and-seek in the early evening light. At first, Ida just watched, but soon she hoisted up her dress and darted around with her friends.

The children slipped back inside when the bride and groom cut the white, three-tiered wedding cake. Andrew Brown's sister, Annie Lane, was serving cake to the children. "Alicia," she said, "I've heard so much about you. Be sure you come and visit before you leave."

"Thank you, I will," Alicia said.

Musicians unpacked their instruments. Tables were pushed to the side. The newlyweds danced a slow waltz.

A catchy jig followed. Young and old flowed onto the dance floor and bobbed back and forth like waves in a small cove, laughing and talking. Alicia danced with Ida and the other children and also with Uncle Arthur.

Late into the night, long after the girls were in bed, the merry music drifted gently over the tranquil village.

YEAST
AND
THE LANDLORD

ANNIE Lane looked up from her sewing machine when Alicia opened the door. "Sit down, my love. I'll have this curtain finished in a minute." Annie pumped the foot pedal vigorously. The needle moved up and down along the seam.

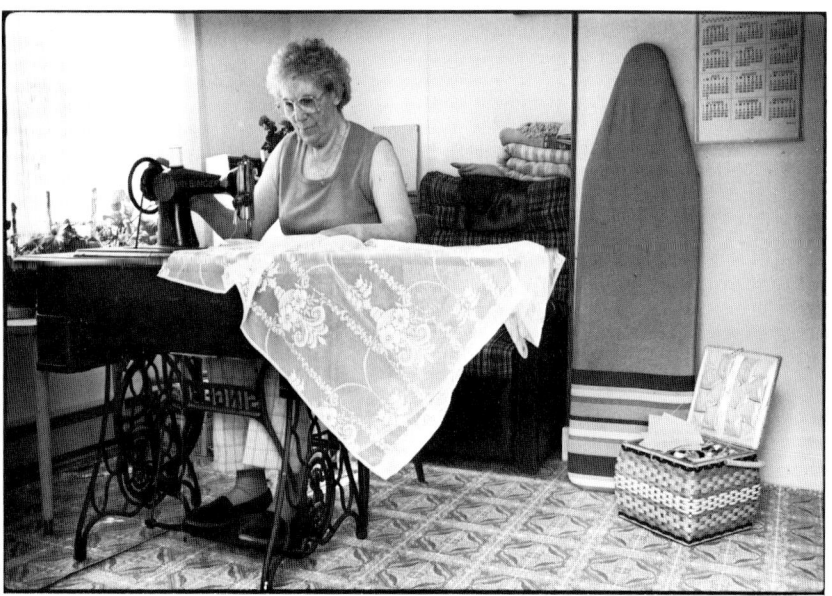

"Did you enjoy the wedding?" Annie asked.

"Yes, it was fun," Alicia said, inspecting the antiquated machine.

Annie cut the thread and folded the curtain. "I'm making bread," she said. "The first batch of dough is rising, and I'm going to make a new batch now."

"Can I help?" Alicia asked.

"I daresay you can." Annie covered her gray hair with a pink nylon scarf and tied an apron over her slacks.

In the kitchen, Alicia slowly poured the bubbly yeast into the flour that Annie had measured into a large mixing bowl. She watched as Annie worked the liquid into the flour with bare hands. Pressing down with her palms, she kneaded it into a soft dough. Satisfied, Annie covered the bowl with a cloth and placed it near another cloth-draped bowl next to the warm stove.

"Now it has to rise."

Alicia slipped outdoors. Roy Lane was fitting a new doorframe on the back entrance to his house next door.

"Fine day today," Alicia said.

"Well, if it isn't the postal assistant!" Roy said. "What are you doing today?"

"I'm raising dough at Annie Lane's house." Pointing to the unfinished wall, she asked, "Your landlord lets you do this?"

Roy laughed. "I'm the landlord. I built this house before I married my bride, Louise."

"You built it all by yourself?"

"The whole family helped. My father showed me how to do it. He had learned it from his father. All the men in the village build their own houses. The women help, too."

Roy worked with saws, planes, and chisels.

Alicia thought of her city apartment that was always in need of repairs.

"Roy, I wish you could come to New York and fix up my place," she said.

"Is Alicia here?" Roy's wife appeared from behind the screen door. She saw the girl and said, "Annie Lane called. She is ready to make the bread."

Annie was waiting for Alicia. "The first batch of dough is ready," she said. She cut a chunk, shaped it, and placed it in a buttered pan. "You can make rolls," she said, showing Alicia how to handle the velvety dough. Alicia beamed. She formed little balls of dough the way Annie had.

While the dough rose one more time, they prepared dinner.

"I'm going to miss the smell of freshly baked bread," Alicia said.

"Goodness, when are you leaving?"

"In about a week. Annie, do you think it's possible I could go out on a fishing boat?"

"I guess my brother Andrew might take you."

"I haven't seen women or girls go out in fishing boats. Ian said they didn't take the ladies."

Annie laughed. "That's because they're busy at home. Ian was just teasing."

When Alicia returned to Ida's house with a bag of crusty rolls, Eileen Brown came over.

"Alicia, Aunt Annie called my dad. He says you can go fishing tomorrow if the weather is good."

"Yeahhh! I can go fishing!" Alicia cried, and danced with her friend around the kitchen table.

. . . .

GOING
TO SEA

ALICIA was up and waiting for Andrew when the night was still fading. A raw wind was blowing and the sea looked unfriendly. Alicia ended up back in bed.

She was leaving in just five days. To her frustration, the weather was just as bad the following three mornings.

Finally, on the day before her departure for New York, early sun brightened the sky in the east. The wind was down. Alicia waited anxiously at the kitchen window. Then she saw Andrew walk toward his fish stage and wave for her to come.

"Are you dressed warmly, Alicia?" he asked.

"Oh, yes." She was wearing just about all her clothes. The layers made her feel like a mummy.

Andrew helped her climb into the gently rocking boat. Alicia sat up front in the bow.

Eating slices of bread, Andy and his cousin Kenny appeared at the wharf. The three men loaded fishing gear into the boat.

Andrew started the engine. For a moment, Alicia's seafaring enthusiasm was dampened by an overwhelming odor of fish and diesel fumes. Then the boat picked up speed, slicing the dark water with its white bow. The houses along the harbor shrunk until they looked like a row of white teeth in the early sun.

Alicia hummed happily in the breeze. At the tiller, Andrew scanned the water. They were approaching the narrow harbor passage.

Hidden rocks lurked close to the water's surface here. A boat could easily smash on the invisible "sunkers," as they were called. But all the Salvage fishermen knew the passage to the ocean like the backs of their hands.

Andy and Kenny snoozed in the stern. Andrew nodded toward his son. "He's fished with me during vacation since he was eight."

They traveled parallel to the coastline. A white buoy danced on the water up ahead. Andrew slowed the engine. They had arrived at the first net.

Andy pulled up the buoy's line until a green net emerged. Father and son picked flounder, a flat fish, out of the mesh. Meanwhile, the boat rolled on the waves, up and down, back and forth. Alicia's stomach felt queasy. Andy and Kenny reset the empty net in the water. Andrew steered the boat to other nets. None produced much fish.

"Andrew, how deep is the water?" Alicia asked.

"About fifteen fathoms," he shouted, but Alicia didn't understand.

In the distance a boat crawled over the swells.

"That's Johnny and Ett." Andy pointed. "They're inshore fishermen, like us."

The boat turned toward a barren island with steep cliffs. While Andy and Kenny worked a mackerel net loaded with shiny fish, Andrew kept the boat from smashing against the cliffs. The pressure in Alicia's stomach increased.

Andrew noticed her pale face. "Are you all right, Alicia?"

She nodded bravely.

"We're heading back now." The engine groaned and picked up speed. She studied the endless horizon.

"It's all water from here to Ireland," Andrew yelled.

"That's where my mother comes from," Alicia shouted. Then she realized that tomorrow, she would be flying home to her mom.

The swells broke into white spray as they entered Salvage Harbor. The houses grew back to size. Andrew dropped Alicia off at his wharf on the way to the fish plant.

Eileen, Ida, Roxane, and Ian came running.

"Did you get seasick, Alicia?" they asked.

"Almost!" she said. "But I'm glad I went."

"This is for the city girl who went to sea," Ian said, and gave Alicia a starfish.

For a while the ground under her feet seemed to sway as she proudly walked home.

The children all knew Alicia was going to leave the next morning, and in the afternoon they swarmed to Ida's house. Laury brought an Instamatic camera. They snapped pictures of one another with Alicia in their midst.

GOOD-BYE,
SALVAGE

IN the evening Aunt Bessie helped Alicia pack her suitcase. After that the family visited with the Browns.

"Andrew, how deep is a phanthom?" Alicia asked.

"It's called a fathom," Andrew said, smiling. "It's six feet, and it's used to measure the depth of water."

"I can't believe Alicia is leaving tomorrow," Violet said. "It seems she only just arrived."

"She's not as skinny now, and her cheeks are red." Grandma looked affectionately at the girl.

Tired from her long and exciting day, Alicia fell asleep on the daybed, her knitting in her lap. The grown-ups drank tea and chatted in the cozy kitchen, and Violet finished the last rows of Alicia's scarf.

The next morning, Alicia went from house to house to say good-bye. At Aunt Mary Jane's she turned back at the door. "There were no raspberries at the old cemetery . . .?" she said.

The old woman smiled. "Not raspberries, my love. Blueberries."

Uncle Arthur lifted Alicia's suitcase onto the pickup. Tearfully she hugged her Salvage family one more time.

They all waved good-bye: Aunt Bessie, the grandparents, Uncle Pearce holding Sarah, Beverly, and Ida, who cried. "Come back next summer. . . . God bless you. . . . Write!" they shouted as she drove off.

Once more, Alicia saw the familiar village. The truck rattled past the last house. Annie Lane waved from her porch.

Traveling with Alicia was a small broom from Heber—just the right size to tuck into her suitcase. It also held raspberry jam from Marlene, crocheted slippers from Aunt Mary Jane, a doily from Grandma, mittens from Violet, a little wooden boat, her mother's scarf, cookies, and shells. Her favorite treasure, the little starfish, she kept in her handbag.

In a few hours she would share all of these presents with her mom, together with her memories of a wonderful summer.

SALVAGE REVISITED:
AUTHOR'S NOTE

I ORIGINALLY documented Alicia Belford's summer in Salvage in 1977. Twelve years later, in 1989, I returned to Salvage to find out if, and how, the community had changed.

Salvage is prospering. The road is now paved and cars are about as numerous as boats. Fiberglass boats are replacing wooden ones, and, in the name of progress, wood stoves are being replaced with central heating systems. The operation of the fish plant has been expanded, and now the fish is filleted and packed there before it is sent out. Many more women—some of them Alicia's former playmates—work there.

Aunt Bessie and Uncle Arthur's family is smaller. Beverly moved with her fisherman husband and two children into their own house. Grandma and Uncle Pearce have died. But Sarah, Ida, and Grandpa, who will soon be ninety, still live at home.

Aunt Mary Jane Heffern died at age ninety-four, and Belle Hancock retired after forty-one years of postal service. But Heber Heffern keeps making brooms, Violet knits, and Annie Lane still bakes the best bread. Fred and Eliol Heffern have retired from fishing, and so has Andrew Brown. Son Andy invested in a long-liner with two fishermen, and they pooled their nets and traps.

The Salvage people are just as hospitable, tolerant, and friendly as ever. Families remain close-knit, with no divorces. Television may have reduced socializing, but neighbors do visit and occasionally go to a dance and have a merry "time." Young men still build houses for their future brides, who will include Alicia's friends Eileen, Ida, and Roxane. A handful of bright students have gone on to higher education. Ian has a degree in computer science.

To the Salvage people, their village remains the most beautiful spot on earth. Alicia Belford, now a young woman, still lives in New York. She is looking forward to her first reunion with her Newfoundland friends at the publication of this book.

A LOOK INTO
NEWFOUNDLAND'S
PAST

NEWFOUNDLAND'S history is as wild as its coastline. The island was inhabited as far back as 2300 B.C. by the Maritime Archaic Indians.

Vikings traveled south from Greenland in A.D. 1000. When they built a few short-lived settlements in Vinland, as they named Newfoundland, the Vikings encountered a people called the Dorset Eskimos. Like the Maritime Archaic Indians, the Dorset Eskimos eventually died out.

The next Europeans arrived accidentally on the shores of Newfoundland in the late 1400s. Explorers from England, Portugal, France, and Spain all sailed to the North American continent on their search for a shorter, western route to China, where they could purchase spices. But instead of spices, they found an abundance of codfish in the waters of the new-found land; and in the rich breeding grounds known as the Grand Banks, located off the southeast coast of Newfoundland, the explorers discovered many varieties of fish. From the sixteenth century on, Newfoundland and the Grand Banks were visited summer after summer by fishing fleets from European countries.

For the Beothuk Indians, who inhabited Newfoundland at the time the Europeans discovered their island, the encounter with the white men proved to be fatal. The Beothuks were soon denied their traditional fishing grounds and were driven inland, where malnutrition and disease diminished their numbers. The last of the Beothuks died in 1829.

The only surviving Indians in Newfoundland were the Micmacs, who sailed north from Cape Breton Island in the mid-1600s in search of richer hunting grounds. Over the centuries Micmacs intermarried with French and English settlers. Some Micmacs continue to live in the interior of Newfoundland today.

In 1583, an English explorer, Sir Humphrey Gilbert, claimed Newfoundland for England. Attempts by British merchants in the early 1600s to colonize the easternmost part of the island failed because of the harsh environment, limited government, and insufficient profits from the seasonal fishing business.

Cod fishing remained the most important occupation. The French, Portuguese, and Spanish processed their catches back in their home ports. The English built stages and flakes on the Newfoundland shores and dried their codfish there. At summer's end, the fishermen returned with their cargo of dried fish to their homeland.

Year-round settlements were discouraged—and, at times, forbidden—by the English for almost three hundred years. Such settlements would have competed with England's summer fishing, and might have lured away able-bodied men who could be recruited into the English navy. Despite that, in the mid-1600s small populations began living year-round in various locations along the coast: French and Basques in the south and west, English and Irish on the north and east coasts.

The early settlers had to cope with brutal weather, plundering pirates, shortages of supplies, lawlessness, and greedy merchants. While they struggled to survive, the English, French and Spanish quarreled and fought battles over territories on the North Atlantic continent.

Salvage—because of its rich fishing grounds, abundance of wood, and sheltered harbor well hidden from passing ships— was the first of the seventeenth-century settlements on Bonavista Bay. The stories of the not-so-good old days were passed down through the generations to people like Andrew Brown.

Life in Newfoundland outports such as Salvage changed little from the early 1800s to the mid-1900s. The men fished for cod in their small boats, dried their catches, and at the end of summer sold the fish to local merchants or those in St. John's. Those merchants were their only buyers, and also the only suppliers of basic food staples and gear. The fishermen had no choice but to trade their fish for often overpriced goods. This system made it difficult for the fishermen to do more than meet their debts, while allowing the merchants to grow rich.

To earn a little cash for their families, fishermen hired themselves out to schooner captains and went fishing in Labrador in the summer, or participated in the dangerous annual spring seal hunt on the ice fields.

Though the fishermen and their families had little or no schooling, they were spirited and tough survivors. Boys worked with their fathers full-time from as early as age eight on. Girls helped their mothers plant and harvest the garden, pick berries, put food up for the winter, care for small livestock, dry fish, carry wood and water, spin, sew, and knit.

In 1855, Newfoundland became a British colony with an independent government. But life in outports like Salvage went on much the same way as before. In larger communities, a nurse looked after the sick. Occasionally a doctor arrived by boat. So did the minister and the mail.

During the winter the men cut wood and hunted. Wood was their only fuel and the only resource available for constructing houses, wharfs, and boats. All fishing stopped during the coldest months of the winter, when the men prepared their gear for the next fishing season. The Twelve Days of Christmas brought a break. Grown-ups and children, masked in improvised costumes, went visiting from house to house, a tradition called "mummering" that survives in many areas today.

Come Easter, the families would check the dwindling supplies in their pantries, and, as Annie Lane remembers, those with a fuller larder would share with the less fortunate.

Outport people were used to living with few material things. There was no electricity or indoor plumbing and few roads at the time of the economic depression of the 1930s. But when the depression reduced the price of fish to a pittance, there was starvation and despair. Many families left Newfoundland and emigrated to Canada and the U.S.

In 1949 the independent-spirited Newfoundlanders voted by a slim margin to become, along with Labrador, Canada's tenth province. Confederation brought badly needed social services: education, health care, and unemployment and retirement benefits.

Electricity was eventually brought to all outports (it came to Salvage in 1963), and telephone service followed soon after. Roads were built and ferry services improved. But for some outport people the new social services carried a heavy price: the government requested that they abandon their remote communities and move to larger places.

Today the traditional way of life of many Newfoundland outports is threatened by high unemployment, the dangers of oil spills from planned offshore drilling, and the continuous overfishing of the breeding grounds in the Grand Banks, which could seriously deplete the stock of fish. Because fish is not as plentiful as it once was, young fishermen like Andy Brown have to pursue their trade with more sophisticated and expensive gear. They may face debt or financial pressures that their inshore fishermen fathers did not have.

Salvage, thanks to the unionized fish plant, enjoys financial stability. The young people stay and raise their families, keeping the social structure of the village intact. But they know that they can only continue to live this independent, traditional way of life for as long as they can harvest the sea.

Andrew Brown now enjoys the financial security of a retirement pension. And if he goes out in his boat to jig a fish, it is for his own frying pan.

• • • • • • • • • • • •

A SALVAGE
FISHING
GLOSSARY

...ANCHOR: A heavy weight, usually made of metal, attached to a boat by a cable and thrown overboard to hold the vessel in one place. (The anchor pictured, used for smaller boats, is called a grapnel.)

...BAIT: Sea snails or pieces of fish or squid attached to a fishhook or placed in a lobster trap as a lure

...BARNACLE: A small, hard-shelled marine animal that fixes itself permanently to a rock, boat, or other surface

...BOAT: FISHING BOAT (also called a skiff). A traditional wooden boat used for inshore fishing; it has an inboard engine but no deck

LONG-LINER. A large fishing vessel with an inboard engine, deck, mast, pilot-house, radar, sonar, and short-wave radio. Used for ocean fishing with a crew of at least two

SPEEDBOAT. A small wooden or fiberglass boat with an outboard engine

...BOAT SLIP: A sloping ramp of wood or stone upon which a boat can be hauled for repair

...BOW OR STEM: The front part of a boat

...BUOY: An air-filled floating object, marked with an identification number, used to indicate the position of nets or traps underwater

...BUOY LINE OR BUOY ROPE: A rope leading from a buoy to a fishing net

...COD, CODFISH: A North Atlantic saltwater fish; since the sixteenth century the principal object of commercial fishing in Newfoundland

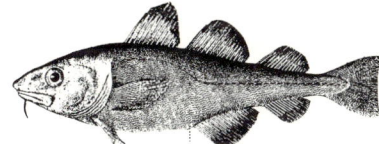

...COVE: A small, sheltered inlet or bay

. . . DRY DOCK: A dock that can be kept dry for use in the construction or repair of ships

. . . FILLET: A piece or slice of boneless fish

. . . FISH BOX: A wooden box with handles used for unloading fish from a boat or washing and salting fish that has been gutted

. . . FISH AND BREWIS: A Newfoundland dish made from hard biscuits soaked in water and cooked with cod and fat pork

. . . FISH FLAKE: A raised platform with wire mesh used for drying salted cod

. . . FISH FORK: A sharp tool with one or two prongs attached to a handle, used to throw fish from a boat to a wharf

. . . FISH PLANT: Factory where fresh fish is cleaned, filleted, packed, and loaded on refrigerated trucks for shipping

. . . FISH WASTE: The inner parts of the fish's body, including the stomach, intestines, and bowel, which are not eaten

. . . FLOAT: An object, such as a piece of cork, attached to the top of a net to keep the net suspended in water

. . . FLOUNDER: A flat saltwater fish

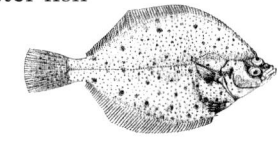

. . . GAFF: A wooden pole of varying length with an iron hook, used to pull or lift objects such as buoys or fish

. . . GALE: A strong wind blowing from 32 to 63 miles (50 to 100 kilometers) per hour

. . . HARBOR: A protected body of water that is deep enough, and sheltered enough, for a boat to be safely anchored

. . . INLET: A small body of water set off from the main body, often as an indented area along the coastline

. . . INSHORE FISHING: Fishing done along the coastline

. . . JIG: To move up and down with a jerky motion

. . . JIGGER AND LINE: Hook and line used for fishing. A curved, weighted hook is baited and lowered into the water on the end of a line.

. . . KNIT: To make or repair a fish net by knotting twine into loops

. . . KNOT: A speed of one nautical mile (a unit of distance used to measure travel by sea or air) per hour

. . . LOBSTER: A large, hard-shelled marine animal with eyes on stalks, two strong claws, and a long abdomen, commonly trapped for eating

. . . LOBSTER BOX: Box or crate anchored in shallow water and used to store live lobsters

. . . LOBSTER TRAP OR POT: A cage with strips of wood for sides and a funnel-shaped net used as a trap for catching lobsters

. . . MACKEREL: A North Atlantic fish that yields a dark meat

. . . MARKER: A wooden floating object, marked with an identification number, used to indicate the position of traps underwater

. . . NET: An arrangement of thread, nylon, or twine knotted together at regular intervals to form a fabric made of loops used to catch fish. The size of the loops varies according to the size of the fish to be caught. The net is suspended vertically in the water with the use of floaters and weights.

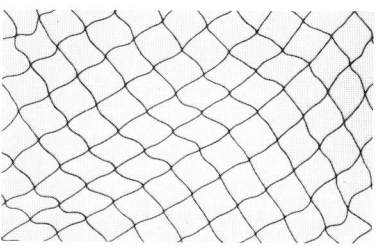

. . . NETTING NEEDLE: Wooden or plastic needle used for knitting nets

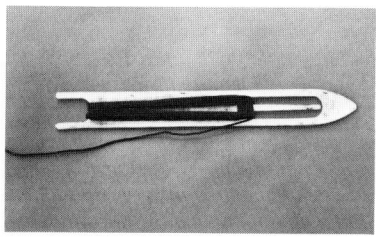

. . . OUTPORT: Remote coastal fishing village

. . . RUDDER: The underwater part of a boat's steering mechanism, to which the tiller is attached; always located in the stern of the boat

. . . SPLITTING TABLE: A wooden table on which fish is cleaned

. . . STERN: The back part of a boat

. . . STORE: A wooden structure, one or two stories high, built on the water's edge and used to store gear and in which to repair gear and nets in wintertime

. . . SWELL: A long, low wave

. . . TIDE: The rise and fall of ocean waters in response to the pull of gravity of the moon and, to a lesser extent, the sun, upon the earth. Tides rise and fall twice in the time between two rising moons, or about every 24 hours and 50 minutes.

. . . TILLER: A bar or beam attached to the rudder to steer a boat

. . . WEIGHT: A piece of lead or other heavy material attached to a fishing line or net to cause it to sink in the water

. . . WHARF: A wooden platform where boats can be tied up for loading or unloading

. . . .

ACKNOWLEDGMENTS

A WARM thank-you to the wonderful people of Salvage for their friendship, hospitality, and help with this book.

A big hug for Alicia and Rosalind Belford. Alicia was a good sport who endured endless photo sessions with patience and humor. Together we share long-lasting, precious memories.

I much appreciate the support from Al Cetta, Carl Parran, Barney Karpfinger, the Marunas family, William J. Lederer, and many of my friends.

Valuable advice for the manuscript was offered by: Barbara Heffern, Andrew Brown, and Annie Lane in Salvage; Jimmy Oldford in St. John's; Gail A. Hogan, coordinator of children's services, St. John's City Libraries; the staff of the Provincial Reference Library in St. John's; and the Canadian Tourist Office in New York City.

I hope that one day, my enthusiastic and patient editor, Cindy Kane, will meet the people of Salvage. Thank you for steering me skillfully through this project. Finally, Cecilia Yung's design turned manuscript and photographs into a handsome book, and I am grateful to her.